• Point Lookout • Point No Point • Pooles Island • Sandy  • Sharps Island • Solomons Lump • Thomas Poin[...] MASSACHUSETTS • Annisquam Harbor • Ba[...]d • Borden Flats • Boston • Brant Point • Butler [...]oge • Chatham • Clarks Point • Duxbury Pier • [...]wn Harbor • Fort Pickering • Gay Head • Hospital Point Range Front • Hyannis • Long Island Head • Long Point • Marblehead • Minots Ledge • Monomoy Point • Nantucket • Nauset Beach • Ned Point • Newburyport Harbor [...] Nobska Point • Palmer Island • Plum Island • Plymouth • Race Point • S[...] • Scituate Harbor • Stage Harbor • Straitsmouth (Island) • Ta[...]nd • The Graves • Three Sisters of Nauset • West Chop • Wings Neck • Wood End • MISSISSIPPI • Biloxi • NEW HAMPSHIRE • Isles of Shoals • Portsmouth Harbor • Whaleback • NEW JERSEY • Absecon • Barnegat • Brandywine Shoal • Cape May • Chapel Hill Range Rear • Conover Beacon • Cross Ledge • East Point • Finns Point Range Rear • Hereford Inlet • Miah Maull Shoal • Navesink • Old Orchard Shoal • Robbins Reef • Romer Shoal • Sandy Hook • Sea Girt • Ship John Shoal • Tinicum Island Range Rear • NEW YORK • Barbers Point • Barcelona • Bluff Point • Braddock Point • Buffalo • Cape Vincent • Cedar Island • Charlotte-Genesee • Cold Spring Harbor • Coney Island • Crossover Island • Crown Point • Cumberland Head • Dunkirk • East Charity Shoals • Eatons Neck • Esopus Meadows • Execution Rocks • Fire Island • Fort Niagara • Fort Wadsworth • Galloo Island • Great Beds • Horseshoe Reef • Horton Point • Hudson-Athens • Huntington Harbor • Little Gull Island • Montauk Point • New Dorp • North Brother Island • North Dumpling • Ogdensburg Harbor • Old Field Point • Orient Point • Oswego Harbor West Pierhead • Plum Island • Point au Roches • Princes Bay • Race Rock • Rock Island • Rondout II • Sands Point • Saugerties • Selkirk • Sodus Light • South Buffalo North Side • Split Rock • Staten Island (Range Rear) • Statue of Liberty • Stepping Stones • Stony Point (Hudson River) • Stony Point (Lake Ontario) • Sunken Rock • Tarrytown • Thirty Mile Point • Three Sisters Island • Tibbetts Point • West Bank (Range Front) • NORTH CAROLINA • Bald Head Island • Bodie Island • Cape Hatteras • Cape Lookout • Currituck Beach • Diamond Shoal Light • Frying Pan Shoals Light • Oak Island • Ocracoke Island • Price's Creek Range Front • Roanoke River • RHODE ISLAND • Beavertail • Block Island (North) • Block Island (Southeast) • Bristol Ferry • Castle Hill • Conanicut Island • Conimicut • Dutch Island • Lime Rock • Nayatt Point • Newport Harbor • Plum Beach • Point Judith • Pomham Rocks • Poplar Point • Prudence Island • Rose Island • Sakonnet Point •

WHO SEES
THE
LIGHTHOUSE?

ANN FEARRINGTON

ILLUSTRATED BY GILES LAROCHE

G. P. PUTNAM'S SONS • NEW YORK

Text copyright © 2002 by Ann Fearrington. Illustrations copyright © 2002 by Giles Laroche. All rights reserved. This book, or
parts thereof, may not be reproduced in any form without permission in writing from the publisher, G. P. Putnam's Sons, a divi-
sion of Penguin Putnam Books for Young Readers, 345 Hudson Street, New York, NY 10014. G. P. Putnam's Sons, Reg. U.S.
Pat. & Tm. Off. Published simultaneously in Canada. Manufactured in China by South China Printing Co. Ltd. Designed
by Gina DiMassi. Text set in Amerigo bold. The three-dimensional illustrations were created on a
variety of surfaces through a combination of drawing, painting, and paper-cutting.   Library of Congress
Cataloging-in-Publication Data Fearrington, Ann. Who sees the lighthouse? / by Ann Fearrington ; illustrated
by Giles Laroche. —1st ed.   p. cm.   Summary: In this cumulative rhyme, lighthouses from around
the United States are observed by one sailor, two pilots, three gulls, and more.
[1. Lighthouses—Fiction. 2. Counting. 3. Stories in rhyme.] I. Laroche, Giles, ill.
II. Title. PZ8.3.F2393 Wh 2002 [E]—dc21 2002000273 ISBN 0-399-23703-8
3 5 7 9 10 8 6 4 2

Blink—flash, flash.

Swirl around, twirl around.
The long, narrow beam
Slices the night.
Who sees the light?

1

One watchful sailor,
Way out on the waves,
Follows the beam
As the sun slowly fades.

Blink—flash, flash.
Swirl around, twirl around.
Who sees the light?

2 Two busy pilots,
Far above land,
Watching the bright light
Circle around.

Blink—flash, flash.
Swirl around, twirl around.
Who sees the light?

3 Three laughing gulls,
Each on her nest,
Bedded down snugly
For a summer night's rest.

Blink—flash, flash.
Swirl around, twirl around.
Who sees the light?

4

Four green turtles,
Wriggling onto land,
Ready to lay eggs
In the warm, damp sand.

Blink—flash, flash.
Swirl around, twirl around.
Who sees the light?

5

Five luna moths,
Drawn to the flame,
Certain the light
Is calling their name.

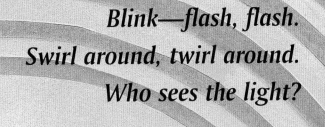

Blink—flash, flash.
Swirl around, twirl around.
Who sees the light?

6
Six giant whales,
Spouting offshore,
Just swimming up
From the cold ocean floor.

Blink—flash, flash.
Swirl around, twirl around.
Who sees the light?

7

Could seven striped kittens,
Out prowling at night,
Searching for handouts,
Could they see the light?

Blink—flash, flash.
    Swirl around,   *twirl around.*
        Who sees the light?

8 Could eight mean pirates,
Each one a ghost,
Sailing their tall ship,
Far off the coast?

Blink—flash, flash.
Swirl around, twirl around.
Who sees the light?

9

Could nine strange creatures,
Living on Mars,
Gazing at Earth,
And counting the stars?

Blink—flash, flash.
Swirl around, twirl around—

10, 20, 30, 40, 50 million miles—

All the way down to . . . .

EARTH!

About Lighthouses

Sailors have always had problems sailing at night. Sometimes they couldn't find the land they were seeking. Other times their ship was destroyed by bumping into unseen land. Erupting volcanoes were probably the first guides for sailors. Around 1000 B.C., the first warning fires were lit on hilltops. About 300 B.C., the Egyptians at Alexandria built the Pharos, history's first recorded lighthouse.

The first lighthouse in the Americas was built at Veracruz, Mexico, in the 1690s. The first lighthouse in the United States of America was built in 1716 at Boston Harbor. It was destroyed in the Revolutionary War.

In 1822 Augustin Fresnel, a Frenchman, developed the Fresnel glass lens that greatly strengthened the beam. England, Scotland, Switzerland, and France pioneered modern lighthouse building and light technology. The USA first developed different flashing patterns to distinguish one lighthouse from another.

The Cape Hatteras Lighthouse (shown on the cover) is the tallest brick lighthouse (213 feet, to top of lightning rod, above sea level—257 interior steps) in the USA. The tower was built in 1870 near Buxton on North Carolina's Outer Banks. In 1873 it was painted with the black-and-white candy-stripe pattern to serve as a distinctive day mark. Fierce Atlantic Ocean storms eroded the sand that separated the Cape Hatteras tower from the waves. In 1998, Congress allocated money to relocate the lighthouse about a half mile inland. The International Chimney Corporation of Buffalo, New York, was awarded the job, which was completed in 1999.

Today, electronics and computers have replaced the job of most lighthouses. Historic, beautiful lighthouses are falling into disrepair. The United States Lighthouse Society, San Francisco, California; the American Lighthouse Foundation, Wells, Maine; the Florida Lighthouse Association, Tampa, Florida; the Lighthouse Preservation Society, Newburyport, Massachusetts; Great Lakes Lighthouse Keepers Association, Dearborn, Michigan, and others work to rescue lighthouses. To celebrate and document the history of U.S. lighthouses, the National Lighthouse Museum was created on Staten Island, New York. This museum is scheduled to open in 2002.

Title page PIGEON POINT LIGHTHOUSE, Pescadero, California. 1872

Copyright page HECETA HEAD LIGHT, Florence, Oregon. 1894

Blink—flash, flash CAPE HATTERAS LIGHT, Buxton, North Carolina. 1803, 1870

Swirl around SAKONNET POINT LIGHT, Sakonnet River, Rhode Island. 1884

1 sailor SPLIT ROCK LIGHTHOUSE, Split Rock Lighthouse State Park, Minnesota. 1910

2 pilots CAPE FLATTERY LIGHT, Tatoosh Island, Washington. 1858

3 gulls ISLE AU HAUT LIGHTHOUSE, Isle au Haut, Maine. 1907

4 turtles SANIBEL ISLAND LIGHT, Sanibel Island, Florida. 1884

6 whales CAPE ANN LIGHTHOUSES (Thacher Island), Rockport, Massachusetts. 1861

7 kittens CAPE FLORIDA LIGHT, Key Biscayne, Florida. 1825, 1855

All the way CAPE HATTERAS LIGHT

Earth! CAPE HATTERAS LIGHT

About Lighthouses RACE ROCK LIGHT, Fishers Island, New York. 1879

Warwick • Watch Hill • SOUTH CAROLINA • Bloody Point Range Rear • Cape Romain Light Station • Georgetown • Haig Point Range Rear • Hilton Head Rear Range Light • Hunting Island • Morris Island (Old Charleston) • New Charleston • TEXAS • Galveston Jetty • Half Moon Reef • Matagorda Island • Point Bolivar • Port Isabel • Sabine Bank • VERMONT • Colchester Reef • Isle La Motte • Juniper Island • Windmill Point • VIRGINIA • Assateague • Cape Charles • Cape Henry Light • Jones Point • New Point Comfort • Newport News Middle Ground • Old Point Comfort • Smith Point • Thimble Shoal • Wolf Trap WEST • ALASKA • Cape Decision • Cape Hinchinbrook • Cape Sarichef • Cape Spencer • Cape St. Elias • Eldred Rock • Five Finger Island • Guard Island • Mary Island • Point Retreat • Sentinel Island • Tree Point • CALIFORNIA • Alcatraz Island • Anacapa Island • Battery Point • Cape Mendocino • Carquinez Strait • East Brother Island • Farallon Island • Fort Point • Hueneme • Los Angeles Harbor • Mile Rocks • Piedras Blancas • Pigeon Point • Point Arena • Point Bonita • Point Cabrillo • Point Conception • Point Fermin • Point Loma Light (New) • Point Loma Light (Old) • Point Montara • Point Pinos • Point Reyes • Point Sur • Point Vicente • Punta Gorda • San Luis Obispo • Santa Cruz • Southampton Shoals • St. George Reef • Table Bluff • Trinidad Head • Yerba Buena Island • HAWAII • Barbers Point • Cape Kumukahi • Diamond Head • Kilauea Point • Makapuu Point • Molokai • Nawiliwili Harbor • OREGON • Cape Arago • Cape Blanco • Cape Meares • Coquille River • Heceta Head • Tillamook Rock • Umpqua River • Warrior Rock • Yaquina Bay • Yaquina Light Head • WASHINGTON • Admiralty Head • Alki Point • Browns Point • Burrows Island • Cape Disappointment • Cape Flattery • Destruction Island • Dofflemyer Point • Grays Harbor • Lime Kiln • Marrowstone Point • Mukilteo • New Dungeness • North Head • Patos Island • Point No Point • Point Robinson • Point Wilson • Turn Point • West Point • GREAT LAKES • ILLINOIS • Chicago Harbor Light • Grosse Point • INDIANA • Michigan City Light Station • MICHIGAN • Alpena • Au Sable Point • Beaver Head • Big Bay Point • Big Sable Point • Bois Blanc Island • Cedar Point Range Rear • Cedar River • Charity Island • Charlevoix South Pier • Cheboygan Lights • Copper Harbor Lighthouse Light Station • Copper Harbor Range • Crisp Point • DeTour Reef • Detroit River • Eagle Harbor Lights • Eagle River Light Station • Escanaba (Crib) • Fort Gratiot • Forty-Mile Point • Fourteen Foot Shoal • Fourteen Mile Point • Frankfort North Breakwater • Grand Haven South Pier Lights • Grand Island East Channel Light Station • Grand Island (North) Light Station • Grand Marais Harbor Range Light Station • Grand Traverse • Granite Island • Gravelly Shoal • Grays Reef • Grosse Ile North Channel Range Front • Gull Rock